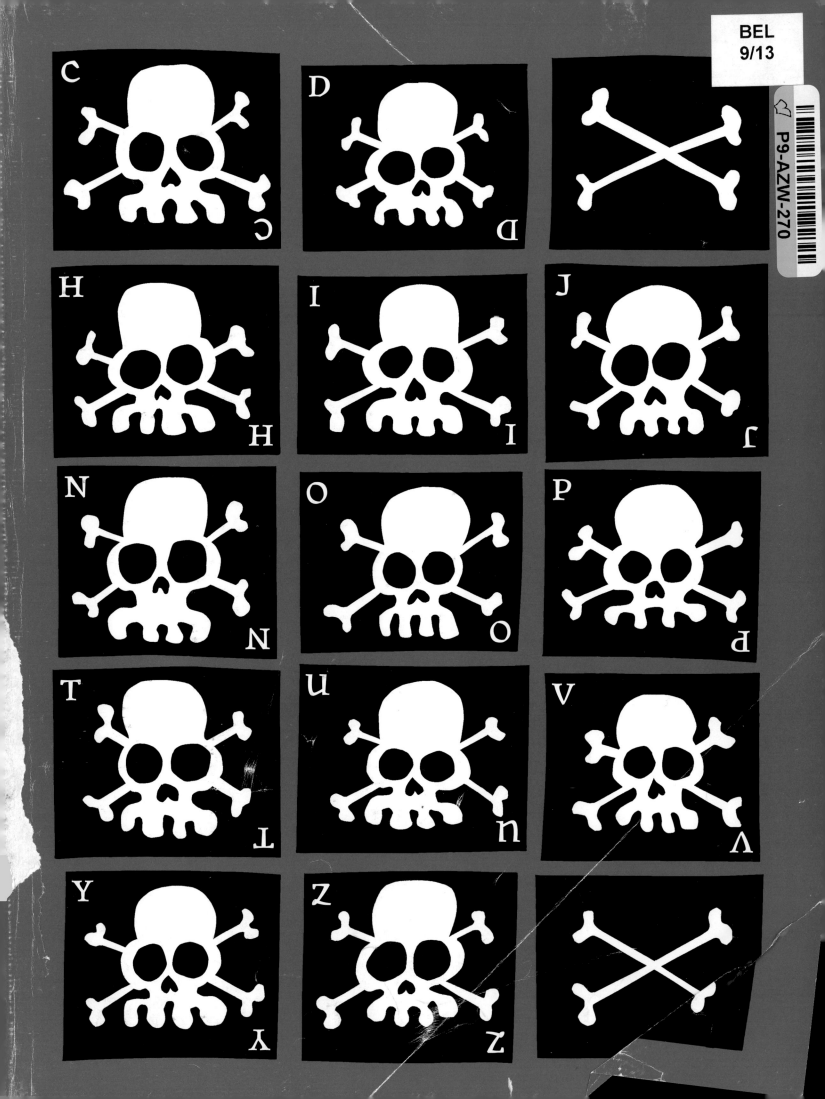

Twenty-six Pirates

DAVE HOROWITZ

Nancy Paulsen Books 🌀 An Imprint of Penguin Group (USA) Inc.

FOR BLACKFOOT.

Thanks to the usual suspects: Nancy, Cecilia, Sara and Annie. Also thanks, in no particular
order, to Frank Zappa, the Beastie Boys, House of Pain, Public Enemy, Simon & Garfunkel,
Dolly Parton, and the H.A.L. 9000. Apologies to Bruce Lee and Roy Scheider.

NANCY PAULSEN BOOKS · A division of Penguin Young Readers Group. ∗ Published by The Penguin Group. ∗ Penguin Group (USA) Inc., 375 Hudson Street,
New York, NY 10014, U.S.A. ∗ Penguin Group (Canada), 90 Eglinton Avenue East, Suite 700, Toronto, Ontario M4P 2Y3, Canada (a division of Pearson
Penguin Canada Inc.). ∗ Penguin Books Ltd, 80 Strand, London WC2R 0RL, England. ∗ Penguin Ireland, 25 St. Stephen's Green, Dublin 2, Ireland (a division
of Penguin Books Ltd). ∗ Penguin Group (Australia), 707 Collins Street, Melbourne, Victoria 3008, Australia (a division of Pearson Australia Group Pty Ltd). ∗
Penguin Books India Pvt Ltd, 11 Community Centre, Panchsheel Park, New Delhi - 110 017, India. ∗ Penguin Group (NZ), 67 Apollo Drive, Rosedale, Auckland
0632, New Zealand (a division of Pearson New Zealand Ltd). ∗ Penguin Books South Africa, Rosebank Office Park, 181 Jan Smuts Avenue, Parktown North 2193,
South Africa. ∗ Penguin China, B7 Jiaming Center, 27 East Third Ring Road North, Chaoyang District, Beijing 100020, China. ∗ Penguin Books Ltd, Registered
Offices: 80 Strand, London WC2R 0RL, England.

Library of Congress Cataloging-in-Publication Data
Horowitz, Dave, 1970– Twenty-six pirates / Dave Horowitz. p. cm. Summary: Twenty-six pirates, one for each letter of the alphabet, demonstrate their
particular—and sometimes silly—talents and skills. [1. Stories in rhyme. 2. Pirates—Fiction. 3. Alphabet. 4. Humorous stories.] I. Title. PZ8.3.H7848Tvp 2013
[E]—dc23 2012023866 ISBN 978-0-399-25777-3
1 3 5 7 9 10 8 6 4 2

Pirate **Arty**. First to the party.

Pirate **Brad**. Born to be bad.

Pirate **Chuck**. Pushing his luck.

Pirate **Doug**. Needs a hug.

Pirate **Earl**. Top of the world.

Pirate **Frank**. Walks the plank.

Pirate **Grant**. Can't.

Pirate **Hal**. He's our pal.

Pirate **Ike**. We also like.

Pirate **Juan**. Wants his mom.

Pirate Lee. Needs to pee.

Pirate **Mark**.... Shark!

Pirate **Nat**. Lost his hat.

Pirate **Owen**. Where's he goin'?

Pirate **Paul**. Cannonball.

Pirate **Quaid**. Not afraid.

Pirate **Roy**. A dangerous boy.

Pirate **Samson**. Awfully handsome.

Pirate Tony. Full of baloney.

Pirate **Ulysses**. Swims with the fishies.

Pirate **Vick**. Feeling sick.

Pirate **Wade**. Mistakes were made.

Pirate **Xavier**. Poor behavior.

Pirate **Yul**. A dancin' fool.

Pirate **Zach**. The final attack.

Put 'em all together
and what do you get?

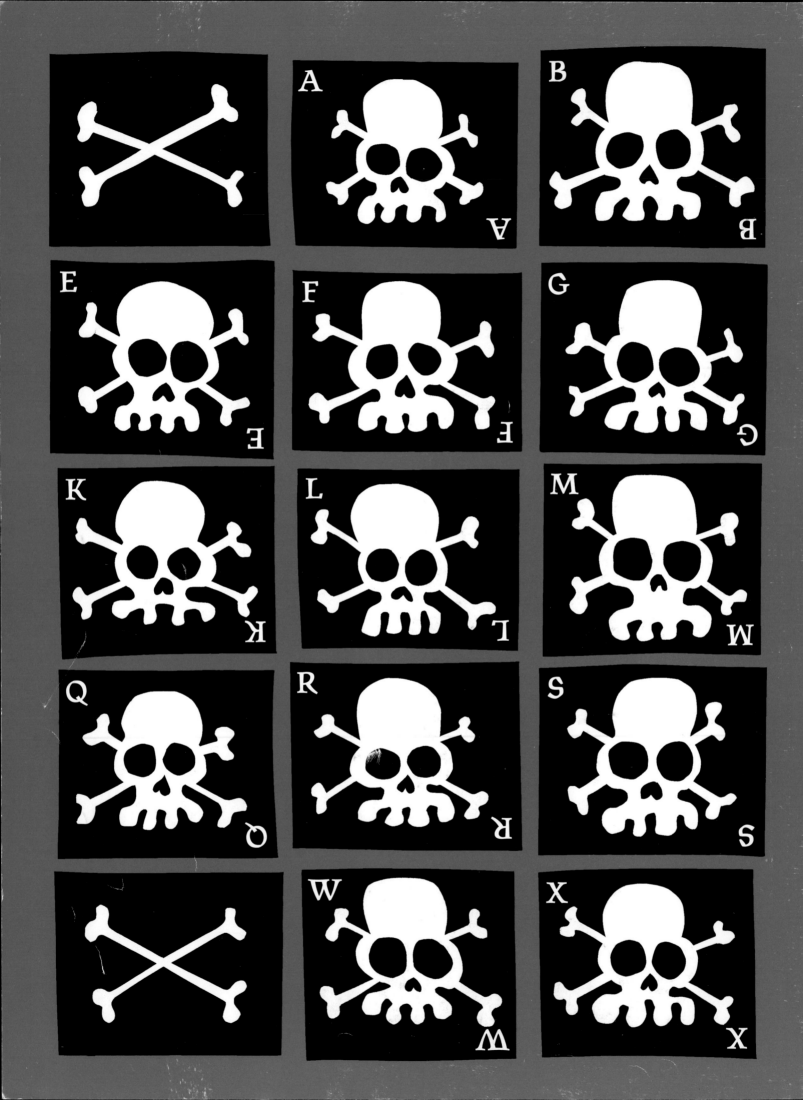